Enid Blyton's

Santa's Workshop

Illustrated by Sue Pearson

Hippo Books
Scholastic Children's Books
London

In the nursery all the toys were getting ready for Christmas. The doll's house dolls were making paper chains, the wind-up sailor was baking mince pies, even Panda was helping to make decorations, and he had only arrived in the nursery three weeks before – a present from the children's Aunt Jane.

All the toys were helping, except for one – the big rocking-horse that lived in the middle of the nursery floor. He was a fine fellow with a lovely spotted coat, a big mane and a bushy black tail.

He rocked back and forth and took the children for long rides around the nursery floor. They all loved him – but the toys were afraid of him.

Sometimes he would begin to rock when they were playing around, and then, how they ran out of the way!

Sometimes he was so proud and so vain that he would not play with the other nursery toys.

"I'm too important to do boring things like making paper chains," he boasted. "I'm the only toy in this nursery big enough for the children to ride on. I ought to be king of the nursery for Christmas."

"Well, you don't deserve to be," said the curly-haired doll. "You squashed the monkey's tail yesterday, and that was unkind."

"I didn't mean to," said the horse, offended. "He shouldn't have left it lying around under my rockers. Silly of him."

"You should have looked down before you began to rock, and you would have seen it," said the doll.

"Well! Do you suppose I'm going to bother to look for tails and things before I begin to rock?" said the horse. "You just look out for yourselves! That's the best thing to do."

But the toys were careless.
Later that morning the little red
toy car ran under the horse's
rockers and had his paint
badly scratched. Next, the
wind-up sailor left his key there
and the rocking-horse bent it
when he rocked on it. It was
difficult to wind up the sailor
after that, and he was cross.

Then the curly-haired doll
dropped her bead necklace and
the rocking-horse rocked on it
and smashed some of the beads.
The toys were really upset with
him about that.

"Be careful, be careful!" they cried. "Tell us before you rock, Rocking-horse! You might rock on one of us and hurt us badly!"

But the rocking-horse just laughed and thought it was a great joke to scare the toys so much.

"You are not kind," said Ben the big teddy bear.

"One day you will be sorry."

And so he was, as you will hear.

It happened that, on the day before Christmas, Sarah and Jack had been playing with their toys and had left them all around the nursery when they had gone for lunch.

Now, the panda's head, and one of his ears were just under the rocker of the rocking-horse. And as soon as the children had left the room the rocking-horse decided to rock.

"Stop! Stop!" shrieked the toys, running forward. "Panda is underneath!"

But the rocking-horse didn't listen. No, he thought the toys were scared as usual, and he didn't listen to what they said. Back and forth he rocked – and poor Panda was underneath!

Oh dear, oh dear, when the toys got to him what a sight he was! Some of his nice black fur had come out, and his right ear was all squashed. The toys pulled him away and began to cry.

"What's the matter?" asked the rocking-horse, stopping and looking down.

"You naughty horse! We told you to stop! Now see what you have done!" cried the toys angrily. "You are really very unkind. We won't speak to you or play with you any more."

"Don't then," said the horse, and he rocked away by himself. "Cree-eek, cree-eek! I'm sure I don't want to talk to you or give you rides if you are going to be so cross with me."

After that the toys paid no attention to the naughty rocking-horse.

They made a great fuss over Panda, who soon stopped crying. Then they went on getting ready for Christmas. Ben wrapped up a present for the pink cat, Rag Doll made a Christmas stocking, and Jack-in-the-Box helped the other toys hang tinsel on the Christmas tree. They had such fun!

In the corner of the nursery, Rocking-horse felt sad. He usually helped hang the tinsel because he could reach higher than the other toys.

"I wish they'd talk to me!" he thought to himself. "I wish they'd play. I'd like to give them each a ride around the nursery – in fact, I'd take three of them at once if they asked me."

But the toys acted as if the rocking-horse wasn't there at all. They didn't ask him to help with anything. They didn't even look at him.

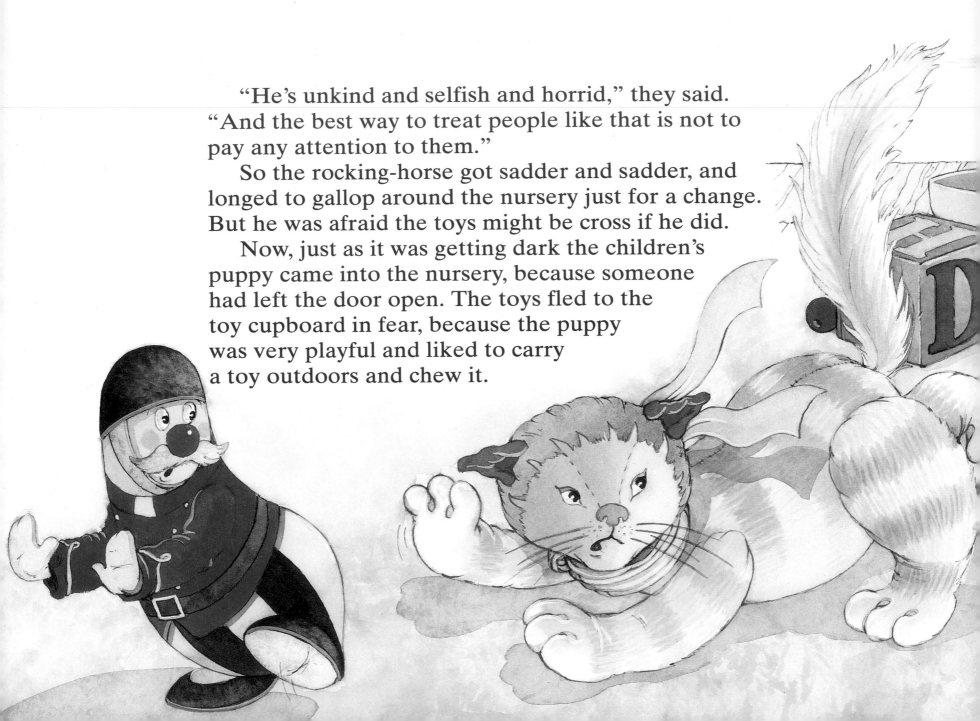

"He's unkind and selfish and horrid," they said. "And the best way to treat people like that is not to pay any attention to them."

So the rocking-horse got sadder and sadder, and longed to gallop around the nursery just for a change. But he was afraid the toys might be cross if he did.

Now, just as it was getting dark the children's puppy came into the nursery, because someone had left the door open. The toys fled to the toy cupboard in fear, because the puppy was very playful and liked to carry a toy outdoors and chew it.

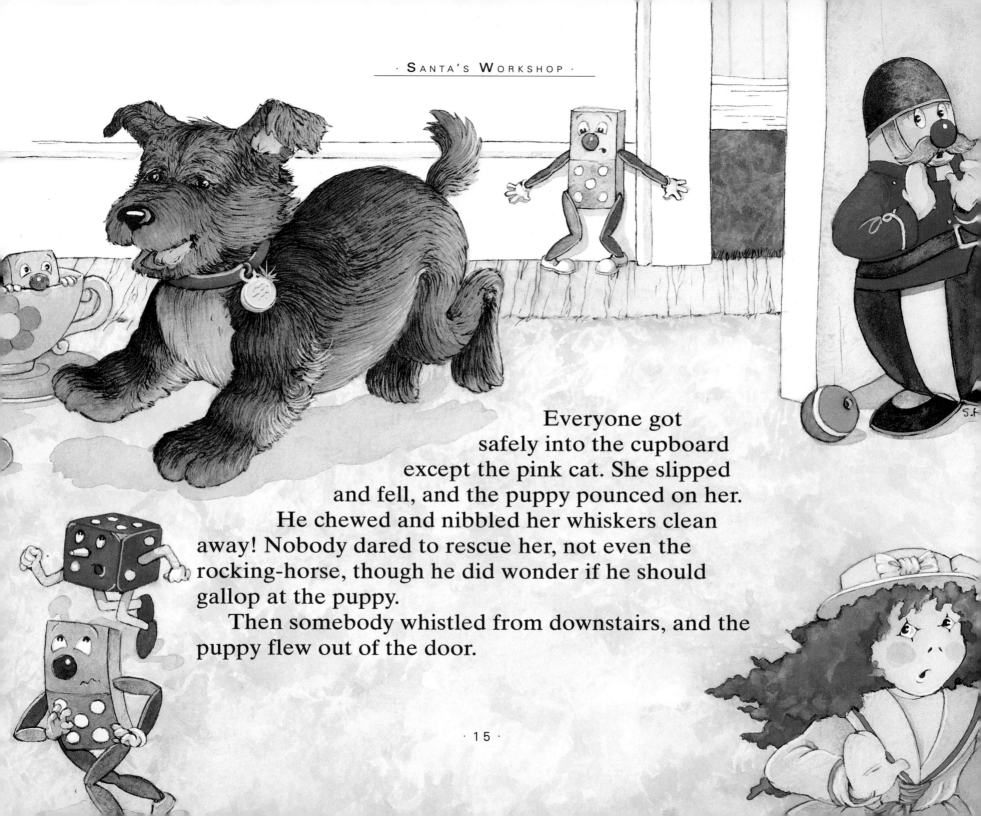

Everyone got
safely into the cupboard
except the pink cat. She slipped
and fell, and the puppy pounced on her.
He chewed and nibbled her whiskers clean
away! Nobody dared to rescue her, not even the
rocking-horse, though he did wonder if he should
gallop at the puppy.

Then somebody whistled from downstairs, and the
puppy flew out of the door.

The poor pink cat sat up.

"Oh!" she said. "Whatever has happened to my fine pink whiskers?"

"They've gone," said Panda, peeping out of the cupboard. "The puppy has chewed them off. There they are, look, on the floor, in tiny little bits."

The pink cat cried bitterly. She had been proud of her whiskers. "A cat doesn't look like cat without her whiskers," she wept.

The sound of the pink cat crying made Panda feel so sad that soon he was crying too.

"What shall we do?" he wailed. "Oh, what shall we do? When Sarah and Jack see us, all nibbled and squashed, they will throw us into the dustbin. Boo-hoo-hoo!"

"Yes," sobbed the pink cat. "They won't want us if they are given brand-new toys for Christmas." And before long the nursery was filled with the sound of toys crying.

How the rocking-horse wished he had not been so unkind! He would miss any of the toys terribly if they were thrown away – and it would be mostly his fault, too! Whatever could he do to earn their forgiveness? He looked around the nursery at all the Christmas decorations and suddenly he knew just what to do.

"Excuse me, toys – but I've got an idea," he said in his humblest voice.

"It's only the rocking-horse," said Ben. "Don't pay any attention to him."

"Please do pay some attention," said the horse. "I've got a good idea. I can take all the broken toys to Santa Claus's workshop. I know the way because I came from there. Perhaps Santa Claus can fix you all and make you better?"

"But it's Christmas Eve!" cried Panda. "Santa will be too busy delivering presents to have time for *us*."

"Oh no!" replied Rocking-horse. "Santa is the friend of every old toy. No matter how busy he is, I'm sure he will find time to help us if we ask him tonight!"

"Well! Let's go then," said the teddy bear. So the toys helped Pink Cat and Panda, Wind-up Sailor and the monkey, Curly-haired Doll and the little red toy car all up on to Rocking-horse's back. Then Ben sat at the very front and said,

"Let's go!"

"Cree-eek, cree-eek!" went Rocking-horse, across the nursery floor and up, away out of the window and into the night sky. For miles and miles they travelled, rocking past twinkling stars towards the great hill where Santa Claus lived.

Luckily for the toys, Santa was at home. He was busy piling a new load of presents onto his magic sleigh. His faithful reindeer would take them fast and far – to the other side of the world in the blink of an eye. When he heard the sound of the rocking-horse neighing and hrrumphing at the door, he came to see who was there.

Rocking-horse explained why they had come and,
to the toys' delight, Santa said he would be glad to
help. He only had three more loads to deliver before
morning. Then he inspected each of the toys in turn to
see what the damage was.

"Dear, dear!" said Santa Claus, looking severely at
the rocking-horse. "I hope you are ashamed of
yourself. I have heard of you and your stupid
ways of scaring the toys by rocking
suddenly when they are
near. Come in!"

The horse rocked in and followed
Santa Claus to his workshop. In no
time at all Santa had straightened
out Wind-up Sailor's key and
mended the curly-haired doll's
broken beads. He soon fixed the
monkey's squashed tail and patched
up the toy car's scratched paint.

Then it was Panda's turn. Santa opened a drawer and looked into it.

"Dear me!" he said. "I've no panda fur left. It's all been used up. Now what am I to do?"

He turned and looked at the rocking-horse.

"You've a nice thick black mane!" he said. "I think you'll have to spare a little for Panda!"

Then, to the rocking-horse's horror, he took out a pair of scissors and cut a patch out of his thick mane! How strange it looked!

Quickly and neatly, Santa Claus put the black fur on to the panda's head. He stuck it there with glue, and it soon dried. Then Santa looked at Panda's squashed ear.

He found a new ear and carefully put it on. It belonged to a teddy bear, really, so it was brown, instead of black, and looked rather odd.

"Now I've no special black paint!" said Santa in a vexed tone. "Only blue or red. That won't do for a panda's ear. Ha, I'll have to take off one of your nice black spots, Rocking-horse, and use it for the panda's ear. That will do nicely!"

He carefully scraped off a large spot on the horse's back, mixed it with a tiny drop of water and then painted it on Panda's new ear. It looked fine!

"Thank you very much indeed!" said the panda, gratefully. "You are very kind."

"Not at all!" said Santa, beaming all over his big, kind face. "I'm always ready to help toys, you know! And how can I help you?" he said, looking at the pink cat. She soon explained all about her whiskers.

"Oh dear, oh dear, oh dear!" said Santa shaking his head sadly. "I'm right out of whiskers."

Just then, a small voice piped up behind him. It was Rocking-horse.

"I should be very pleased to give the toy cat some of the hairs out of my long black tail," he said. "They would do beautifully for whiskers."

"But how can we get them out?" said the pink cat.

"Pull them out, of course," said the horse.

"But it will hurt you," said the pink cat.

"I don't mind," said the horse, bravely. "Pull as many as you like!" So Santa pulled eight out, and they did hurt. But the horse didn't make a sound.

Then Santa carefully gave the cat her whiskers back.
"One whisker!" he said. "Two whiskers! Three whiskers! Oh, you will look fine when I have finished, Pink Cat. These are black whiskers, long and strong, and you will look very handsome now." And so she did. Very fine indeed!

At last it was time to go, so all the toys clambered back on to the rocking-horse.

"Thank you Santa," they cried as they left. "Thank you for helping us all."

Then off they went home again, rocking hard all the way in order to get home by morning, and glad to be good as new again.

The toys cheered when they saw them.

"What glorious fur you have – and look at your fine new ear!" they cried when they saw Panda. "And look at your lovely whiskers," they said to Pink Cat.

Rocking-horse said nothing. He stood in the middle of the nursery floor, quite still, not a rock left in him.

"Santa took some of Rocking-horse's hair for me, and one of his spots to paint my ear black," said Panda. "You can see where he has a bare place on his mane, and one of his biggest spots is missing."

Sure enough, it was just as Panda had said.

"I must say it was nice of the rocking-horse to give you them," said Ben, suddenly.

"And to give me my new whiskers," added Pink Cat. "Especially as we haven't even spoken to him lately. Very nice of him."

All the other toys thought the same. So, they went over to the rocking-horse who was still looking sad.

"Thank you for taking us to Santa's workshop," said the curly-haired doll.

"It was very kind of you," said the monkey.

"I can't thank you enough!" said the pink cat. "I had pink whiskers before, and they didn't show up very well – but these show beautifully. Don't you think so?"

"You look very handsome," said the horse. "Very!"

"Your tail looks a bit thin now, I'm afraid," said the pink cat. "Do you mind?"

"Not a bit," said the rocking-horse. "I can rock back and forth just as fast when my tail is thin as when it's thick. You get on my back and see, Pink Cat!"

So up got the pink cat, and the rocking-horse went rocking around the nursery at top speed. It was very exciting. You may be sure the horse looked where he was going this time! He wasn't going to rock over anyone's tail again!

"Oh, thank you!" said the pink cat, quite out of breath. "That was the nicest ride I ever had!"

"Anyone can have one!" said the horse, rather gruffly, because he was afraid that the toys might say "No," and turn their backs on him.

But they didn't. They all climbed up at once.

"Nice old horse!" they said. "We're friends again now, aren't we? Gallop away, gallop away!"

And you should have seen him gallop away again, around and around the nursery until the sun peeped through the curtains.

"Merry Christmas, Merry Christmas," they heard the children shouting.

"Good gracious," said Ben the teddy bear. "It's Christmas Day!" All the toys had quite forgotten.

And a lovely Christmas Day it turned out to be, too. Sarah and Jack were amazed at how smart all their old toys looked – apart from Rocking-horse, whose mane and tail looked a bit straggly.

"Never mind," said Sarah. "We will always love you, toys, even if you are old and worn, won't we Jack?"

"Oh yes," said Jack. "Merry Christmas toys. Merry Christmas to you all!"